D1496017

Bridging the Gap

Maria Anderson

Cover design, illustration, and book design
by Amanda Hughes

Published by The Wrighting on the Walls, LLC

This book is for those who do the work to make a better version of themselves.

Michelle,

Invest in the relationships that bring you joy. You may be surprised by their value!

Maria
- 2021

Also by Maria Anderson

Learning to Love Yourself:
A 10-Day Commitment to You

The Other Side of Fear, Book One in
The Other Side of Fear Trilogy

CHAPTER 1

"**H**ow will you rebuild the relationships?"
I have re-read this question over and over again in the last week.

I honestly don't see the connection between this and my healing when it comes to Virginia.

I like Dr. C but sometimes her homework makes absolutely no sense to me and doesn't seem relevant at all.

Dr. Courtney or "Dr. C," as I like to call her, is my new therapist. After our trip to Boston, I realized just how much the past was holding onto me in the present.

When we came home, I did a ton of research on therapists in Atlanta. I checked the educational background, medical reviews, customer satisfaction scores—anything I could get my hands on that would give me some insight into the type of care I could expect from the doctor that was going to fix me.

I needed a therapist who would be relatable and objective. One who would help me to look on the positive side. But one who would also be down to Earth and tell me like it is... whether I wanted to hear it or not.

I may or may not have cyberstalked and found Dr. C's social media pages, which was not easy. I needed to see the person behind the medical degrees. Once I found her profile, I knew she was the one for me. Any therapist who rocks Adidas and a Kangol hat on the weekends has to be cool. In my head, she low-key jams out to Barclay Crenshaw when no one is looking.

My homework from our last session is to work on a plan for how I can go about starting the process to rebuild my relationship with Virginia's sons, Allen and Derrick.

Allen is the one closest in age to me; I guess he is technically the "middle child." I can imagine having a relationship of some sort with him. We've spoken a few times in the last decade or so and each interaction was pleasant. But most importantly, Allen doesn't seem to hate me, which makes him a winner in my book.

Derrick is Virginia's firstborn, so the eldest of the three of us. I don't know much about him except the last time I saw him he gave me a death stare that still gives me goosebumps. Have you ever heard the expression "If looks could kill?" My one and *only* interaction with Derrick over the last decade was the inspiration for that expression. I did not get warm and fuzzy from him; instead, I got "run for cover and don't look back."

Focus, Renee. Back to the homework assignment.

"I will commit to communicating with Allen, in some form, at least once every other week."

There! Dr. C will just have to accept that answer.

In our therapy sessions, Dr. C has so many "creative suggestions" for what my communication with Allen should look like. She loves to ask, "Is that enough to bridge the gap with your brothers?"

I roll my eyes and correct her, "Virginia's sons."

***

CHAPTER 2

A little more than a year ago, after the kids and I accompanied my husband, James, on an incredibly intense trip to Boston, I made the bold step to call, Allen. It was like a blind date but on the phone. The call was so awkward! There was lots of silence and neither one of us really knew what to say.

During that first call, we did the normal "catching up stuff." Allen gave me a brief overview of the last fifteen years of his life—work, wife and kid.

I gave a similar and brief overview; I didn't want to seem too braggy or show-offish. The only time the conversation was not awkward was when Allen proudly doted on Allen Junior, AJ, who is a star high school basketball player. I could literally hear Allen Senior smiling through the phone, which was refreshing.

Tonight, the dinner table is surrounded by James, my son, Alex and me.

London, my daughter, is at her best friend's house planning for the city science fair competition next week. This year's project is something about the various chemical compositions of candles and why some smell better than others for a longer period of time. My basement is covered in wax, essential oils and small pieces of leftover wick. My sweet girl is going to rock the science world one day and very soon.

"I spoke to Allen on my way home today," I say, passing the mac and cheese to my husband.

"Oh really? That's twice that you spoke to him this month," James says, incredulously.

"Yeah, AJ is a small guard, on his basketball team. I guess he's kind of a big deal," I reply, ignoring James' disbelief.

"Small guard? Mom, did you just say, 'small guard?'" Alex interjects looking at me sideways, sounding confused and disgusted at the same time.

"Yeah. Isn't that a position?"

"No, Mommy it's not. Do you mean 'point guard?'"

"Sure, I guess. Allen may have said something

about that, too." I say and shrug my shoulders, annoyed by the interrogation about basketball positions. The important part is not what position the boy plays, it's about my conversation with his father. But my basketball-obsessed kid only hears basketball-related terminology.

James and Alex shake their head in disbelief at my mix up.

"Anyway," I continue with a slight eye roll. "I told Allen that maybe we could try to catch one of AJ's games this season. Maybe during another business trip."

Because the last one was so successful, I think to myself.

Alex is ecstatic at the idea of going to Memphis. He and James start going down a basketball history rabbit hole. Both Alex and James become animated, hands moving everywhere with excitement as they discuss big games. Their voices are getting louder and louder, recalling memories of shots heard around the world by players that would forever be memorable.

"Chris Garner!" James shouts with excitement.

"Lou Williams!" Alex adds in while pretending to shoot a roll back into the basket as if it was a basketball.

Almost as if they were in sync, both yell "Anfernee Hardaway!"

Now that is a name that I know!

I giggle with a crooked smile as I think about myself as a teenager with my best friend Nicole chasing the Orlando Magic bus around what used to be called "The Boston Garden."

We paid a ridiculous amount of money to watch Anfernee "Penny" Hardaway play our beloved Celtics. We dressed in our Magic jerseys and spent the entire game screaming his name. Nick Anderson, another Magic player, became so annoyed that he turned around and told us two loud teenage girls to "shut up." We looked at him, rolled our eyes, flipped our sideways ponytails and continued yelling for Penny. Oh, to be young and carefree again!

"Mommy!" Alex calls my name which pulls me back into reality. "Did you hear my question?"

"No, Alex, I'm sorry."

"When are we going to visit your brother, Allen? Is it okay if I call him 'Uncle Allen?' He is my uncle, isn't he?"

The kids are trying to wrap their heads around having two uncles that they've never met. For as long as they can remember, the only person I have ever called my brother was Rob.

My brother Rob still lives close to Boston and he Facetimes the family and me regularly. Our kids are so close, they are more like brothers and sisters than "first cousins." Having Rob as a big brother has been the one constant in my life since I moved in with Grandma.

I've spoken to him at length over the last few months about rekindling the relationship between Virginia's sons and myself. He is just like Grandma—always encouraging and protective.

I remember when I first mentioned the whole "bridging the gap" idea to Rob. He did a great job of trying to be supportive and hiding his uneasiness. Rob was around for my childhood; he saw the impact of broken promises by both Virginia and my father. But he also saw that I survived the broken promises and went on to build the life that I had always wanted as a child. At the end of the conversation, Rob reminded me that regardless of what happens with Virginia's sons and me, he would always be my big brother.

"Alex, you can call him whatever respectful name that you are comfortable with and I am not sure when we're going. But here is AJ's cell phone number; I got it from his father today so that you guys can stay in touch with each other."

"Awesome!" Alex shouts, jumping up from the table and running for his room to call AJ. He halts at the door. "I'm sorry, can I be excused?"

James and I chuckle. "Of course. Clear the table, please."

Relishing the silence and ambience, James and I sit at the table a little longer, sipping our glasses of wine. One of London's candles flickers on the table creating a warm glow to the room. She named this one "Boston" in honor of our trip last year. It smells a lot like the ocean. The scent of the candle is so spot-on that it takes me back to the beaches at home. I can feel the breeze on my face and hear the sound of seagulls off in the distance.

There are so many words being spoken through looks, glances and slight touches.

My husband truly gets me. He understands the anxiety, the nervousness of the unknown and the doubt that lies beneath this gap between Allen and me.

None of that matters right now. I give James my sexiest smile, finish my wine, squint my eyes and seductively bite my lip. "Should we head to bed, my love?" I alluringly ask my partner in crime.

"Hell yeah!" he replies.

We laugh softly as he grabs me and lands a soft kiss on my forehead—always my protector.

He smacks my butt as I turn to walk up the stairs—always my lover.

***

CHAPTER 3

Alex and AJ hit it off immediately! Typical teenaged boys, they didn't spend a lot of time on the phone actually talking but lots of time texting. I thought Alex's fingers were going to catch on fire the day Steph Curry hit 102 shots during practice.

Neither London nor I could see the big deal. I mean, why would anyone want to take 102 shots at once? Sounds a little like overkill to me, but what do I know about basketball? Nothing.

Allen and I have continued our awkward "bridging the gap" conversations. We both say that we need to get the kids together so they can meet each other. But neither one of us has actually made any plans.

We'll get there one day.

Alex and AJ, on the other hand, have been behind the scenes working hard on a plan to get us to Memphis. I swear those two are worse than the telemarketers who keep calling about a "car warranty" for a car that I don't even own. After Alex and AJ nagged us for months, both Allen and I basically had no choice but to plan a trip.

Fast forward and Memphis, here we are!

***

This weekend AJ has a big game versus a rival high school. Apparently, it's a full week of events leading up to this one game. I think Alex and James called it "March Madness" but for high schools. Again, I don't know much about basketball, but this must be a big deal based on the full hotel capacity when I tried to book our room. Allen mentioned that college recruiters would be at the game. Apparently, AJ really wants to go to the University of Memphis so his performance this weekend is extremely important.

James is wrapping up a seminar in Chicago and will join us in Memphis tomorrow.

Hmm. I need to remind him to bring me a two-piece from Harold's #1. Everyone knows the original Harold's is the best! That place has the best fried chicken in the mid-west!

***

This trip to Memphis is a huge step in me attempting to rebuild my relationship with one of Virginia's sons. I really am committed to doing the work. I want to let the past go and build a brighter future. I was excited to share my plans for the trip with Dr. C.

"Will Derrick be there?" Dr. C said with one eyebrow sort of raised and a half smile on her face. She leaned in just a little more and her head was tilted to the side as if we were getting to the climax of the session and she didn't want to miss a detail of my answer.

"Um, I don't think so. Allen hasn't mentioned anything about Derrick."

Allen would have mentioned if Derrick was coming. Right? I am not mentally prepared to deal with Derrick. Allen would have definitely mentioned it. At least I hope that he would have.

I am going to Memphis, to "bridge the gap" with one of Virginia's sons. One is better than none.

I can't even lie and say that I have been doing any work towards bridging the gap with Derrick. The gap between us is much larger for reasons that have always escaped me. I clearly remember him staring at me at Virginia's makeshift funeral. There was such intensity in his eyes as he glared at me. A weird mixture between disdain, anger and sadness. I'm honestly not sure if there is a bridge wide enough to cross the rift that exists between us.

Rebuilding the relationship with Virginia's son is going to take many steps, one at a time, perfectly calculated. This trip to Memphis is one small step. I am taking a step towards getting to know one of her sons. I'm just not sure this is the trip to take multiple steps, including interacting with her other son.

Our flight into Memphis was smooth taking off and landing. I had a session with Dr. C yesterday, so I'm not as nervous as I would expect for this trip. As I follow the GPS directions to the hotel, both the kids and I are in awe of the city around us as this is our first visit to Memphis. The downtown skyline is sporadically filled with tall buildings; the airport is full of cars and people, as expected. The drivers here seem friendlier than the ones at home, which is good because the Dr. Martin Luther King Jr. Expressway has so many twists and turns, winding and intersecting components much like they do in Atlanta. Except, I have no idea where I'm going so I appreciate the grace being offered to me from the other drivers also leaving the airport. As I drive, I notice that the landscape along the highway varies from tall buildings to factory type buildings and even some abandoned or run-down homes. Based on the variations in the scenery, it is easy to tell that Memphis has an interesting history.

After a relatively short drive, the kids and I check in to the Peabody Hotel. As always, London has done some research on her own about Memphis. Apparently, our hotel has famous ducks that parade throughout the lobby on a daily basis. Before we head to dinner with Allen and his family, London has requested that we make our way to the lobby to experience a piece of Memphis' history.

I appreciate the innocence of this experience as I admire the joy in London's face as she watches the ducks splash around the fountain after their "parade." I also can't help but wonder how ducks keep getting incorporated into our trips. First, we were on plastic ducks touring Boston, and now we are watching real ducks do their ducky thing in our hotel in Memphis.

I hope this isn't some weird omen.

The trip to Boston was emotional. I am anticipating the trip to Memphis to be a breeze in comparison. It's a weekend filled with basketball and meeting Virginia's youngest son, who I don't really know, and his family. Like I said, awkward, but a breeze, nonetheless. I mean, Allen and I are close in age, both calm in demeanor and family orientated. We just fell out of touch for almost two decades. Life gets busy. Days and years go by so quickly. Yet, even threw the distance of time we always tend to be friendly with one another when we speak.

I'm actually excited to meet his wife, Nelle. She's a Howard graduate, Real Estate Lawyer who sounds down to earth and likes to have fun. Reminds me a lot of myself. I'm hoping she'll make the interactions between Allen and I less delicate.

The kids and I spend thirty minutes in the lobby before heading out to meet Allen and his family for dinner.

I am trying to be in a positive mindset about this dinner, but just in case I am going to start working on my fake smile now. I should have grabbed a drink from the bar during the parade to give me some liquid courage. But it's just Allen and his family—I should be fine!

Let the fun begin. Again.

***

CHAPTER 4

Thanks to the GPS, we arrive at the Brazilian restaurant pretty quickly. Allen and his family are seated at the front waiting for us when we enter the building.

"Hi, Allen," I say as we enter through the front door and I spot the familiar man sitting with his family.

Allen and I exchange a weird combination of uncomfortable hug-handshake.

"Renee, this is my wife, Nelle, and my son, AJ." Allen says.

"Hey, girl!" Allen's wife says as she grabs me in an embrace that feels familiar, warm and tight. Very tight! Nelle has a genuinely warm personality. I think I am going to like this woman.

I just need her to loosen up a little with the hugs.

"Hi, AJ, nice to meet you. I've heard so much about you," I say, trying hard to escape Nelle's death grip. "This is my son, Alex, and daughter London."

Alex and AJ have some secret handshake like they've known each other for years and have spent an abundance of time together. Nelle scoops Alex up quickly into a bear hug—*so this is something she does with everyone*. Alex wiggles away from Nelle to give Allen a pound.

London gives Allen and Nelle a hug, fully prepared for the intense embrace, while giving AJ a fist pound.

This place is extravagant in décor with unique floral arrangements strategically placed throughout the restaurant. There is a huge flower centerpiece in the middle of the dining room which immediately draws your attention. The intense color of the flowers is stunning. The kids are mesmerized by the constant stream of servers carrying what appears to be meat on a stick. The aroma of the food and the ambiance are enticing.

"Is your party ready to be seated?" the hostess says with a Southern drawl.

"We're waiting on three more, but we can be sat if the table is ready." Allen replies.

Did he just say three more? It must be some of

AJ's friends.

"So, we flip the coin, and the servers will just keep adding meat to our plates?" Alex asks our server, pointing to the two-sided coin that is located at each of our seats. He's completely in disbelief, bubbling over at the idea of having endless access to food. The server explains how the coin is used as a signal for the food servers to bring a variety of marinated meat options to the table.

"Yes, you help yourself to the salad bar and when you are ready for the meat, you simply flip your coin over to the green side. When you have had enough, you simply flip your coin to the red side." The server smiles at my son, who has just mentally entered heaven.

"Oh, I am never flipping to the red side!" Alex says excitedly as he reaches to flip his coin to signal the food servers.

"Um, before you flip that coin, Mr. Ready to Eat This Place Out of Business, you must go get some veggies first." I warn, bursting Alex's bubble.

"Same goes for you," Nelle tells AJ. "And you as well, Mister," she says, looking at Allen.

Right as Allen does a horrible job of pretending to be ashamed, in walks someone whose face I recognize but seeing it here feels out of place. The light brown eyes and tall stature.

That's definitely Derrick. But how? Why?

Derrick is looking around the restaurant when two adorable young girls exuberantly point at our table. "Daddy, Uncle Allen and TiTi Nelle are over there," the two girls say in unison.

Alex and London call my best friend "TiTi Nicole," too; I guess all the young kids have decided to call Aunties this new name.

As Derrick's attention lands on my face, he blinks quickly multiple times. He straightens his back as he walks to our table with what looks like reluctance. Obviously, my presence here is a surprise to him as well.

I shoot a glance at Allen that lets him know I am surprised... and not in a good way. We will definitely talk about this later.

"Hey, Bro," Derrick says as he smiles, hugs and gives his brother a secret handshake.

Did I just see him whisper something into Allen's ear?

"Hey, Bro, glad you and the girls could make it. And where are my beautiful nieces?" Allen replies.

"Right here, Uncle Allen," The girls reply as Allen pulls them in for a hug.

"Nelle, looking as beautiful as always. I will never understand how my brother snagged a woman like you." Derrick says as he hugs Nelle.

"It was just his lucky day," Nelle replies. She

and Derrick chuckle.

Derrick slowly makes his way around the table toward our end. "Hello, Renee," he says as if someone were pulling the words from between his clenched teeth. There is no bending over to hug me or the kids. Just a stiff walk to the other side of the table where he takes a seat and releases a deep breathe, as if he is working hard to control himself. The room suddenly feels much warmer than it did a little while ago.

"Hello, Derrick," I reply with my fancy fake smile and my unbothered tone.

"Are these two your kids?" Derrick says as he adjusts himself in the chair right across from me.

"Hey," Alex gives a head nod. "I'm Alex."

"And I'm London," she says with a quick wave.

In the most sarcastic tone I may have ever heard, Derrick tells Alex and London, "You two have gotten so big since the last pictures that I've seen of you."

Shots fired! Okay. Maybe I haven't sent Virginia's sons the latest family Christmas cards but seriously?!

"Derrick, are these two beautiful young ladies your girls?" I ask, trying to be friendly and working the hell out of my fake smile.

"Oh yes, this is Maya and Aaliyah, my little queens," he replies.

"Hey, I'm London!" London says to Maya and Aaliyah.

"Hey!" the girls reply back.

"What's up? I'm Alex." Alex takes a break from his conversation with AJ to speak.

"Maya and Aaliyah, I know you've never met her before, but this is your Aunt Renee," Derrick emphasizes the "never" as he leans back in his chair with a smug expression on his face.

Shots fired again! Okay, I see how this dinner is about to go. Derrick is obviously trying to push buttons or make me feel guilty about our non-existent relationship, but I won't fall for it.

"Hey girls! It's great to meet you." I mean, technically I'm not lying. I am happy to meet them. Their father is a different story.

The server returns to take our drink order.

I am definitely going to need some liquid courage for this dinner.

London, Maya and Aaliyah bond over their love for limes in their water. I overhear London say, "It's so much better than lemon" while Maya and Aaliyah screech in excitement, simultaneously responding "that's what I say."

Meanwhile, I do my best to avoid making eye contact with Derrick. I can feel his death stare as I interact with everyone else at the table. I can also hear his heavy sighing when I answer questions from Nelle or Allen. Part of me wants to ask him if he has a problem but I know this isn't the time or the place. So, for now, I will sit back, enjoy dinner and ignore the angry bull that thinks my red shirt means "charge."

I have to admit, the food is nicely seasoned, and the bartender did a great job with the drinks.

At least I was right about one thing: Nelle definitely was a great buffer.

The guys are all deep in basketball talk. Lebron versus Michael Jordan, who's the greatest. I've come to learn that this is an ongoing debate for every basketball fan.

I interrupt with my answer to their "all important" question. I suggest that Magic Johnson is better and imagine my surprise when Nelle backs me up without hesitation, like she totally believes in my obviously ridiculous opinion.

This sends Allen, AJ and Alex into an uproar. Derrick shakes his head, but it felt differently; I can't explain the feeling, it was just cold and unwelcoming.

"You have no idea what you're talking about," Allen tells me.

"She doesn't even speak basketball," Alex reveals.

They go on and on about how Magic Johnson is "good" but he is no match for Jordan and definitely no match for Lebron.

Nelle and I have tears running down our faces as we are laughing so hard at their dramatic response. Nelle and I leave them to their sports talk and have a great conversation about the latest reality television foolishness. Reality television is my guilty pleasure that allows me to escape reality every so often.

Aaliyah, Maya and London have been talking nonstop; it is truly a thing of magic watching them eat and talk so quickly. It's so interesting how these kids have never met but they act like they've known each other their entire lives. London tells Aaliyah and Maya about her latest project, the candles, and they are amazed by her talent. The girls talk about everything under the sun, moon and stars combined. Music. Boys. The coolest places to shop locally. At some point in the night, I notice that London lets Maya borrow her sweatshirt when she gets cold.

It's refreshing and encouraging to see the kids getting along so well.

I wish I could say the same for the adults.

Allen keeps attempting to make small talk between Derrick and me; it feels like he's trying to strike up a conversation between us. So far tonight, it's safe to say that I've exchanged more words with my local grocery store cashier than with

Derrick.

Derrick provides single worded, usually smug, answers, without ever making eye contact. He even makes an occasional grunting noise instead of responding with actual words.

I start to roll my neck and my eyes, but I maintain my fake smile and continue having the conversation with Allen.

Derrick orders three more drinks while Nelle and I are still nursing our original.

The kids are trying to order additional banana desserts when the server brings the check and leaves it on the center of the table.

"I'll take care of that," I say as I grab the bill. I have zero desire to waste time sitting here being stared at by Virginia's son just to break up the bill according to what everyone ordered.

"Are you sure?" Allen asks.

"Absolutely," I reply. "It's the least I can do."

"Thank you," Both Nelle and Allen reply.

Derrick mumbles something under his breath. It definitely didn't sound like "thank you," but I wasn't expecting one from him.

We exit the restaurant, all three of Virginia's kids with their kids. What a sight to see.

Allen and I do the awkward hug, handshake, head nod thing. Nelle gives me another bear hug. Without so much as a head nod or semi-hug, and through clenched teeth, Derrick and I mumble a quick "bye" to each other. Everybody heads toward their cars to leave for the night. Derrick had quite a few drinks tonight. I sure hope that he's being safe and taking the girls home in an Uber.

And here I thought we were going to have a nice, simple family dinner. Nope, it seems like nothing involving *my family* can be simple. Instead, what I received was a warm welcome from one of Virginia's kids and the biggest non-verbal altercation that I have ever experienced with the other.

***

The kids and I arrived back to the hotel and I couldn't wait to call James and tell him about Derrick.

"Renee, it couldn't have been that bad," James says on the other end of the phone.

"No, James, you're right—it was worse. He's so smug and condescending.

"If he didn't want to be in the same room with me, I don't even know why he bothered to stay when he saw me. His body language was clear, he hates me, and I'm cool with that, but he better watch himself."

The words are coming out of my mouth faster

and faster, my Boston accent getting stronger and stronger. That typically happens when I'm angry. I continue like that for several minutes.

"I know that pompous ass said something smart when I paid for the check. But I didn't see him pulling out his wallet to pay for anything."

I sip my Moscato and continue to vent about the disaster of a *simple* family dinner. This glass of wine is much needed after *that* dinner.

James lets me vent, knowing that I simply need to get it all out.

"Babe, I'll be there tomorrow. We can go out on the city and sightsee. Just the four of us."

"That will be nice. I can't wait to see you. I really need you."

"Oh, you need me. And how do you need me?" he says seductively.

"Boy, stop! I'm supposed to be angry." I giggle at my husband's silliness.

"I love you, babe, and you are stronger than anything or anyone that comes at you."

"I love you, too, and thank you for the reminder."

We hang up and instead of sneering angrily, I have a smile on my face. I don't know how that man does it, but he makes the world a calmer place for me. When Hurricane Renee is headed to category 5 status, James is the calm, cool water that brings me down to a tropical storm.

***

CHAPTER 5

"**I**'m on the road, I'll be there in seven hours." I instantly feel overcome with peace as I read the text James sent this morning.

I start doing the math in my head. Left at 5:00 am, should be here by 12:00 pm, I am definitely looking forward to seeing my husband. He is my support in every single way.

I take a sip of coffee the kids ordered from room service and I am grateful that my kids are early risers and understand the benefit of room service. They know enough not to get Kevin from *Home Alone* crazy, but they never forget their mommy when they order for themselves. My kids learned early on that Mommy needs coffee to get the day moving.

I hear the kids in the parlor watching *Black Panther* for the millionth time. We finally found a movie that the whole family can agree is amazing and watch over and over again. Wakanda Forever! I am not quite ready to get out of bed yet, so I turn on the TV and find an episode of *Law and Order SVU* that I've probably seen a few dozen times.

Lying in bed, I can't help but to think about last night.

Last night was interesting. I let Derrick get to me, but I hope I hid it well. I can't let him irritate me like that again; he's not worth it. I have to remember that I am here to bridge one gap, one step at a time.

I know that Allen has no ill will so I'm guessing he had the best of intentions when he invited Derrick to the dinner last night. He just wants everyone to get along. But he definitely should have talked to both of us first and let us make the decision to see one another.

I need to stop thinking about last night. I take another sip of coffee and watch Tutuola, and Liv solve the case.

My phone vibrates, disturbing my quiet time.

"Hey, Renee!" I hear the voice of Nelle on the other end of the phone.

"Nelle? Hey," I say, completely caught off guard. *Who calls someone this early in the morning?*

"What's up?"

"I was thinking it would be cool to go sightseeing. Allen and I have some time today while AJ practices for the game. What do you think?"

I think it's too early for all of this planning shit.

"Umm. I would love to, but James is coming in soon and I want to be sure we're here when he arrives."

"Oh! I can't wait to meet him. We can definitely go when he gets here. I know your brother will love to have another man around to take some of the heat off." Nelle laughs at her statement.

Great, what excuse can I make now?

"I would love for you guys to meet James," *No I wouldn't.* "But we'll have to play it by ear. You know he may be tired from the drive."

And I don't want any more surprises.

"I totally get that. I'll check back later in the day. Maybe we can grab lunch or something."

"That sounds good."

"Yay! I'm so excited. Talk to you later."

I'm left staring at the phone. *Did that really just happen?*

Okay, maybe the dinner wasn't as uncomfortable for everyone as I imagined it had been. The kids definitely hit it off. London even let Maya keep her sweatshirt. Probably because Maya subconsciously started chewing on the extra-long sleeves while the kids were engrossed in conversations about some rapper YM something.

What if we go on this tour with Nelle and Allen only to be surprised again? I had enough surprises last night. I am definitely not up for anymore today!

I lie in bed trying to process dinner and the phone conversation with Nelle while the television plays in the background. Maybe this is Nelle's way of trying to extend an olive branch. I couldn't have been the only one who noticed Derrick's body language and the energy he was giving off at dinner last night. Derrick laughed with everyone but me, and his hands were animated when he talked to everyone else... but me. He clearly enjoyed the conversation as he engaged with the rest of the table. Just not with me.

Whenever Allen tried to include me in the conversation, Derrick instantly sat back in his seat, took a sip of his drink and stared intently. Almost as if he were trying to find an untruth in my words.

Actually, he took a lot of sips of his drink and he had a lot of drinks. He reminds me so much of Virginia.

I'm going to take a hot shower and throw on some casual clothes and sneakers. Maybe the kids and I will see what's close to the hotel until James

gets here.
>But first, let me check his location.
>Yeah, we have a few more hours.

***

CHAPTER 6

The kids think the hotel is incredibly fancy and decided to speak with fake English accents the whole time we ate brunch at the Lobby Bar. After brunch, we laid around the room; the kids focused on their phones and I was engrossed in my latest book *Always Remember November*. Much to mine and the kids' delight, James arrived shortly after we returned to our suite.

I was hoping James would want to do sightseeing as a family, just the four of us, as he mentioned the night before. I should have known he would be willing to adjust our plans as soon as I mentioned the call from Nelle. After all, family is extremely important to James. He wouldn't have let me come this far to rebuild my family only to slink back at the slightest hint of trouble. Even if the trouble was like warm water encouraging Hurricane Renee to surface. I can hear Dr. C in my head, "Bridge the gap with your brothers, Renee. Do the work." I roll my eyes just thinking about the work that needs to be done and mentally correcting her. "Virginia's sons."

***

I give my fake and cautious smile as the elevator doors open on the first floor. I tilt my head to the side when I spot Allen and Nelle watching the ducks.

So far so good, no Derrick to be seen. Wait, let me scope out the bar since it appears Virginia's son likes to have a drink or two. Nope, still no Derrick. We may be good this time.

Nelle grabs me into another tight hug as we approach. Allen and I semi-hug, you know the one arm around the waist, tap with the hand, last all of 10-seconds hug. I'm still cautious as I greet Allen and Nelle, waiting for Derrick to appear out of nowhere.

I introduce James to them; I forgot to warn him about Nelle's tight hugs. I smirk a little at his "oh" when she grabbed him in. The kids and I softly laugh at James' response.

"So, where are we off to?" I ask Nelle, who is beaming from ear to ear.

"Let's start with FedEx Forum. I know Alex is a huge basketball fan. We can talk about the sites, get some drinks and wrap up with some famous Memphis barbecue."

"Sounds good." *Sounds exhausting.* "Let's roll."

As we approach the FedEx Forum, I can't help but wonder if *this* is why FedEx increased their shipping costs, this place is enormous!

The brick exterior of the building fits in perfectly with the buildings around it. The basketball team is away this weekend, so the streets are quiet and uneventful. I can imagine the streets when the team is home, bustling with people, music and souvenir vendors. Allen, James and Alex talk about the latest in the NBA world. Nelle, London and I discuss the latest episode of the *Real Housewives* of some random city.

As our next stop, we head toward the historic Beale Street.

I'd heard that Memphis was a major blues spot but hearing and seeing the beauty of the blues intertwined into every piece of Beale Street history is absolutely beautiful. I watched a movie based around Beale Street a few years ago but seeing the street in person is a different feeling.

The vibrant blue "Beale Street Memphis" sign welcomes us to an area that is rich in culture. The neon signs aren't lit now but they line the street, labelling the restaurants, bars and venues along the way. A low humming of music swims from every doorway we pass. Sweet sounds of trumpets and trombones exposing the musicians' deepest emotions for all the world to hear. Enticing you to come inside and hear more of their stories told through the music. Allen points out numerous spots that come alive at night, full of rhythm, dance and drinks. James and I make a mental note; this is definitely a good spot for adult time.

As we walk and enjoy the unique buildings that surround us, Allen tells us the history behind the different landmarks. We approach Beale Street Baptist Church, which was built by free slaves, and the place where Ida B. Wells wrote and printed *Free Speech*, an anti-segregationist paper. As I stare at the tall cream building, I can't help but think of the conversations that were held here. Conversations that would lead to change for the betterment of our people. The architecture of this building is stunning. The tall arch doorways. The perfectly placed circle of windows. Simply stunning.

We drive by the National Civil Rights Museum, which includes the Lorraine Motel, and sit in silence as the weight of the location weighs on every piece of our spirit. The history that lives in this place is mesmerizing. It's getting later into the evening, so we don't have the time to go in and visit today. London is, of course, upset by this, but we promise that it is a must do before we leave.

Allen and Nelle insist that we have dinner at a local restaurant, because according to Allen, it has the best barbecue in Memphis. I ask if we're going to Rendezvous; I watched a show on the Food Network that featured several of their dishes. Both Allen and Nelle agree, the food is good there, but they reassure me that the food at *Cozy Corner* is to die for. We pull up to a square building with a bright blue border and a sign that looks like it has seen better days. The ambiance is definitely different from the fanciness of the Peabody Hotel, but the way the smell of barbecue hits my nose as we enter the doorway should be a crime!

Is that Wonder Bread?! Oh, my gods of hickory smoked bliss! Any place that serves Wonder Bread with their barbecue knows what they are doing.

"Does that menu say *Barbecue Spaghetti*?" James asks, his words laced with excitement and anticipation.

"Why yes, hun, yes it does," I reply.

"What do you suggest?" James and I ask in unison, sounding like Maya and Aaliyah from last night.

"Anything," both Nelle and Allen reply.

We have enough food on the table to feed a small Army—if that Army consists of a growing teenage boy and two men who think they are still growing.

During dinner, London tells Nelle and Allen about her latest science experiment. They are so impressed with her second-place finish in the city science fair. But London won't be happy until the State competition is complete and she places in the top. Nelle suggests that London could sell her candles as a business, taking her project to the next level. London definitely likes this idea; I can see a spark in her eye and the wheels start to turn in her head.

Alex shares about the joys of being a freshman in high school and his love of everything basketball. Allen starts a huge debate when he asks Alex about his top five NBA players of all time. London, Nelle and I laugh as Alex defends his choices against the "old heads," Allen and James.

Tonight's dinner is much more relaxed. The laughter is genuine. The smiles are real. The atmosphere is light and friendly.

This is a simple family dinner.

During dinner, while the conversation is flowing, James looks at Allen, shaking a rib bone in his hand, mouth full of food and tells him, "Bro, this was a great suggestion. This rib is so damn good." We laugh at James' endorsement and agree—just with less food in our mouths.

We eventually find the energy to push away from the table and head back to the hotel. Nelle grabs a to-go plate for AJ to enjoy after practice.

When we get to the hotel, goodbyes are less awkward.

Alex imitates his dad, "Uncle Allen," pretending to hold a rib bone and have a mouthful of food, "that place was great. Thank you for the tour."

"Uncle Allen," I guess Alex has decided on a name to call my brother.

James rolls his eyes at Alex as we all laugh in response.

"That is your child, Renee," James replies.

"But he looks just like you," I reply with a wink and a smirk.

London prepares herself for a "Nelle hug" and says, "Thank you for the advice about the candles. Goodnight, TiTi Nelle."

I guess the kids are getting used to the idea of having another uncle and aunt. I prepare for the anticipated bear hug from Nelle. How does such a small woman hug so tightly?

James, Alex and Allen exchange some weird

dude handshake.

Allen walks over to me and gently gives me a real hug, the kind with two arms. "I'm so glad you're here and you totally have mom's laugh."

This last statement makes me pause. I hadn't heard that before. I don't remember her laugh, voice or much else anymore.

"Hun, you okay?" The sound of James' voice brings me out of my thoughts.

"Yeah. Got caught up in my thoughts for a moment there," I reply. "Thank you guys for taking us on a tour and wrapping it up with that delicious food." I say trying to sound normal, but my head is foggier than it was a few moments before.

"Oh, girl, you know I'm a foodie. I'm glad y'all enjoyed it," Nelle replies. "We'll see y'all tomorrow. Don't forget to wear your red and black for the game."

"Oh, yeah, that's right." James says.

"Go Bulldogs," I reply.

Allen and Nelle head home and we turn to go into the hotel. James wraps his arms around my shoulders. "That was really fun," he says as he holds me and guides me into the elevator.

"Yeah, it was." I reply.

I laugh like Virginia. Interesting.

***

CHAPTER 7

As I walk towards the bar to meet everyone else, I overhear James talking to someone.

"I won't tell you it'll never happen. I'll just say don't push her too much. Renee addressed a lot of stuff head-on last year in Boston which led her here to you. Let Derrick and her work out their relationship on their time."

"I hear ya, and I can tell that you care about my sister. Obviously, you know her far better than I do, so I'll have to listen to your advice," I hear Allen reply. "I just wish we could all get along like normal siblings."

"Yeah, I get it. But they have stuff they need to work out and they can't be forced."

"Practice patience. Got it."

Glasses cling in agreement.

Wow! My husband and my brother having a heart to heart. Isn't this lovely?

"Hello, gentlemen," I announce myself. "Fancy seeing you here."

"Hey, Babe," James says as he kisses my forehead.

"Hey, Renee," Allen says as he stands to give me a hug. "Nelle is in the powder room."

"Nope, I'm back and it looks like I'm right on time," Nelle announces herself.

"Hey, Nelle."

Prep for the hug.

"Hey, sis," I say, smiling as she wraps me in her snug embrace.

"Is everyone ready?" Allen asks.

"Yeah, the kids are already there. They wanted to spend time with AJ before the game started," I tell Allen and Nelle.

"Let's go cheer on the Bulldogs!" Nelle replies.

The high school gymnasium is more like an arena, massive in size. I can smell the concession stand food as we pass by headed to our seats. The smell of the freshly made popcorn, the pretzels being warmed in the case and the constant sound of drinks being poured. As we enter the gymnasium, I notice that this place is jam-packed from floor to ceiling with students on both sides for the two rival schools. The red and black Bulldog students are loud and ready for the game. The student crowd has gone all out to show their support for the school, including the eight shirtless students in the front row, each with a respective letter painted on their chest, spelling out B-U-L-L-D-O-G-S.

I spot Alex chatting with some Bulldog cheerleaders. My freshman baby is getting way too much attention from these high school girls wearing these itty-bitty cheerleading uniforms. I try not to go into overactive momma bear-mode and snatch him away. But I will be watching them *very* closely.

I search the gym for my other child, hoping there isn't a science experiment happening in the midst of all this craziness. I finally spot London sitting with two young girls who look familiar. *Is that Maya and Aaliyah?* If Maya and Aaliyah are here, then Derrick is probably here. Yup, there he goes, Virginia's son who hates me more than Spike Lee hates the Lakers. I guess I should have assumed he would be here. Maybe I should have gotten here earlier so we don't have to sit with him.

When he spots me, I can see his body language change to a more rigid stance. Well, I am glad to see that he's as excited to see me as I am to see him.

Fortunately for us, there doesn't seem to be enough room on the row where he's sitting for James and me to join.

"Hello, Derrick," I say as warmly as possible. "This is my husband, James. James, this is Derrick."

Virginia's son.

"Hey, good to meet you, man," Derrick replies with a semi-human, even warm response.

So, he just hates me? Good to know.

"Nice to meet you, too, man." James replies, caught off guard from the warmth of the introduction.

I introduce Maya and Aaliyah to James, and they pause their conversation with London long enough to say "hi."

James and I sit in front of the girls while Allen and Nelle sit the row behind them with Derrick.

Allen and Nelle have gone all out with support for AJ: bullhorn, bedazzled school gear, matching sneakers and all.

The girls are paying about as much attention to this game as Nicole, my childhood friend, more like sister, and I did back in the day. They take breaks in between to yell AJ's name, but there is no Nick Anderson here to tell them to "shut up."

I've watched a few games over the years, mainly during the finals with James and Alex, but being in person is a completely different story. The energy in the crowd is infectious. I find myself literally jumping out of my seat when AJ makes a dynamic play. AJ does one of those plays when a teammate passes him the ball mid-air and he dunks it. The crowd goes absolutely wild! Several times throughout the game, James, Alex, Allen and Derrick yell in unison "and one!" It took me a while, but now I realize that means an additional point added to the score.

The Bulldogs definitely came to play but the Spartans did as well, and they are keeping this game tight.

The clock is ticking away, and the game is coming to a close. The Bulldogs are down by two and one of AJ's teammates starts bouncing the ball from the middle of the court. As he makes his way closer to the net, it seems like time has stopped moving around us but in actuality, it is just a few seconds. The teammate passes the ball to AJ, who is immediately rushed by Spartan players... but not before he shoots the ball. AJ falls to the court from the hit but the ball floats in the air and falls into the hoop. Everyone in the crowd, including me, yells "AND ONE!"

His Bulldog teammates help AJ up off the floor and he heads to the free throw line for his one chance to win the game.

SWOOSH!

As I've heard James say so many times before, "like butter, baby."

The crowd erupts and the Bulldog students storm the floor! Everyone in our circle high fives, joining the excitement erupting all around us. Me and Allen. Me and Nelle. Me and James. Me and Derrick.

Me and Derrick.

Not. The realization of what almost happened seems to dawn on Derrick almost as immediately as it does on me, and we hurry to turn away, continuing the high five celebration with everyone around us.

The players and fans celebrate their well-deserved win with a tsunami of student pride, the court overflowing with what seems like every high school student in Memphis.

We let AJ enjoy the limelight with his friends. If the college recruiters are not impressed by this kid's skills, they are crazy.

After some time, the crowd starts to thin out and AJ finds us still in the stands waiting patiently for the school's most popular athlete.

After congratulatory hugs and kisses, we decide to head to dinner to celebrate.

Great, another dinner.

Hopefully the awkward non-high five between me and Derrick won't be a "thing" during dinner, causing his attitude to be even more sour towards me.

One can hope.

***

CHAPTER 8

Everyone arrives to the restaurant around the same time and we are seated almost immediately.

The Bulldogs' star player is recognized as he walks to his seat with his girlfriend, Kerrie, by his side. We were able to talk with his girlfriend a little during the game. She seems like a nice young lady. Definitely has her head on straight. She is going to college in the fall to study Education. She wants to be a high school reading teacher and help students in low-income neighborhoods.

The server comes and takes the drink and appetizer orders for the entire table.

When the drinks arrive, Allen calls attention

for a toast. "To AJ, what a way to celebrate your senior year of high school. Your mom and I are so proud of you, not just because you are an amazing basketball player but because you are an amazing young man. And tonight, you have your Uncle Derrick, Aunt Renee and Uncle James here to celebrate with you. Here's to family, growth and celebration."

Glasses clink as everyone cheers. I inwardly roll my eyes. *Growth.*

Orders are in and we're laughing, the conversation is flowing, and appetizers are holding everyone over until the main course arrives.

"Okay, AJ, it's pretty clear you have a great career in basketball ahead of you. Who are your favorite players?" Derrick asks.

"Penny is definitely one of my favorites." AJ replies.

"MINE, TOO!" Derrick and I say at the same time. We look at each other with a suspicious side eye.

"Mommy, you actually know who Penny Hardaway is?" Alex asks.

"Yes, son. I'll tell you about the time that TiTi Nicole and I went to a game," I reply.

"I can only imagine the trouble you two got into," James says, incriminatingly.

I smirk. *He has no idea.*

AJ continues to name his favorite players, but I honestly haven't heard a word. Derrick also loves Penny Hardaway. And we said it at the same time. I actually have something in common with Virginia's son.

That's interesting.

Before long, the server arrives with our dinner. "Lobster Ravioli, no tomatoes and extra sauce," she says.

"That's me," both Derrick and I say at the same time. Again.

"You take it," Derrick says to me.

"Thanks. No tomatoes and extra sauce, huh?" I reply.

"Yeah, tomatoes are gross."

Something else that we both agree on.

Again, interesting.

As soon as the plates arrive, dinner commences. The conversation lessens as everyone focuses on their entrees. The food is delicious; however, I don't know what I said or did, but I can feel Derrick staring at me again. Maybe it isn't me. Maybe the vibe I'm picking up on has more to do with the string of drinks he's downed. He's working on his fifth now.

The check arrives after desserts and this time James grabs it.

"Wait, Renee paid for dinner her first night in," Allen says while reaching unsuccessfully for the bill.

"Right. We can't have you paying for two big dinners," Nelle says while also unsuccessfully reaching for the bill.

"I insist. Consider this our gift to AJ on a game well-played," James replies, holding the bill to his chest.

"Well, thank you both very much. You're far too generous," Allen responds.

"Yeah. Far. Too. Generous," Derrick says with each word dripping in disgust. It was almost like he meant to say it to himself, but he definitely said it out loud.

I catch myself roll my eyes and snap my neck in his direction. Ready to ask him what the fuck is his problem?

But then I feel James' hand squeezing my thigh. "Let it go," he whispers into my ear.

I look at James with an obvious *He Got me Messed Up* look on my face. Eyebrows raised. Head slightly tilted. Eyes narrowed.

James simply hands the payment to the server and plants a kiss on my lips.

We file out of the restaurant without any other snide comments from Derrick. Lucky for him.

Everyone says their goodbyes, hugs, fist

bumps, customary dude grips and air kisses.

There is still the truthful and emotional I don't like you, you don't like me "bye" exchanged through clenched teeth between Derrick and me.

James and I head to the car, Alex and London walking in front of us. Holding my hand, James whispers into my ear "I'm proud of you, Renee."

"I'm not sure why," I reply, my Boston accent a little thicker than I meant. "He had one more slick comment and it was going to be a problem."

"That's why I'm so proud of you. You're taking the steps." He plants a kiss on my forehead as he closes the car door for me.

On the way back to the hotel, I lean my head back into the car's headrest and remind myself that I shouldn't have to see Derrick anymore this trip. Virginia's son will not ruin this bridging the gap trip. I won't allow it.

Allen and I are making great progress. Derrick's stubbornness will not derail the work we've done.

The sounds of Erykah Badu play on the radio, reminding me that all I must hold on to is me.

***

CHAPTER 9

Daylight seems to come so quickly when we're on vacation. James and I lie in bed, watching *Law and Order SVU*. He loves this show as much as I do and will watch episodes with me even if he's seen them before. The kids have once again ordered room service, including my coffee. I can tell that James has something to say but he also knows I need my coffee first.

"While we were waiting for you yesterday at the bar, Allen mentioned having a barbecue today. You know, to celebrate AJ's big game, let the boys spend more time together, play in the pool, you know—whatever."

"Whatever, huh?" My reply slightly laced with

annoyance. I take a sip my coffee.

"What's up with the attitude, Renee?"

"Who's going to be at this barbecue?" I take another sip trying to swallow the attitude that I can feel building up.

"I don't know. I didn't know that I needed to vet the guest list."

"Hell, yeah you did." I maybe said that with a little too much attitude. *Come on, man!* I think to myself and make a mental note to soften my tone. My beef is not with James. This is not about us. This is about Virginia's son and his disrespectful ass.

"What's going on with the attitude? It seemed like you, Allen and Nelle were getting along good."

Now this man knows they are not the problem! Control the tone, Renee.

"Allen and I are definitely a work in progress toward being in a good place. I like Nelle. She hugs a little too tightly for me but she's cool."

"Nelle damn sure has a tight grip when she hugs," he says, and we both laugh.

I continue, "But you do know that things are not a work in progress with Derrick and me. I think it was pretty obvious last night that he has some underlying issues with me *or alcohol.*" I shrug. "Regardless of who has the problem and what that problem is, at this time, I am choosing not to interact with him if I do not have to."

"I did notice that the atmosphere was a little thick between you and him last night." James says softly as if he's trying to soften the blow.

I snap my neck to look at him sideways. *Did he say, "a little thick?" That is an understatement.*

James reaches for my hand and strokes it gently with his thumb before continuing. "But I don't want you to miss an opportunity when it's presented. Remember, you can only control your emotions."

Yeah, yeah, yeah, I think to myself and try not to show it on my face. "He reminds me of her."

"Who?"

"Virginia."

"Why?"

"The drinking. I mean we all have a drink or two but the only thing that stops him from having another one is the bill that he hasn't offered to pay yet." *Okay, I didn't have to add in that last part but damn he irritates me.*

I can feel my body tensing up as the conversation continues. I don't like this feeling. I don't like not having control of the situation. I definitely don't like the interactions that I've had with Derrick so far.

I sip my coffee and try to regain control over my emotions and my mind. James gives me the space I need to process the conversation. And the time to speak out of truth, not anger.

"Renee, I'm your husband and I love you, so what I am about to say, I'm saying with nothing but love."

Here we go, I'm sure James is about to say something that I really don't want to hear. I put my coffee mug on the nightstand and cross my arms to prepare for whatever he is about to throw at me. I can feel my neck still tilted towards his and I am trying really hard not to roll my eyes, more than once.

James continues, ignoring my clearly defensive body language, "You haven't spoken to your brothers in decades. You don't know what has happened in that span of time. Give them grace and give yourself grace."

"Brother and Virginia's son," I correct him. *Dammit, I hate it when he's logical. And why the hell are tears falling down my face?*

James holds me in his arms and doesn't say a word. Enough has been said. We lie wrapped in bed for what feels like hours. Time is negligent when *Law and Order SVU* is on and I am in my husband's arms.

My phone vibrates.

"Hey sis. Here's the address for the house: 1914 Meadow Ridge Trail. Can't wait to see you guys later. Love Nelle."

Another text rolls in, "Don't forget your bathing suits. And come right in." Smiley face emoji.

I roll my eyes and turn back to the TV.

I guess we're doing this.

***

CHAPTER 10

As we pull up to Allen's house, I can't help but admire the house; it is absolutely gorgeous with the perfect balance of house and nature! It is clear that the builders took great care in the architecture and the look of the building they were creating. The driveway is large enough for us to pull up and not crowd the cars already parked here.

As we exit the car, we hear music playing, water splashing from the pool and you can smell the food cooking on the grill.

I can't lie, I love a good burnt hot dog so I'm lowkey excited. But still weary.

"Hey, TiTi Né. Hey, Uncle James." AJ yells at us from outside as we walk in the front door.

TiTi Né? Okay. I've been called worse.

"Hey, y'all." Nelle comes towards us giving her customary big tight hug. As she hugs the kids, she tells them, "Y'all can change upstairs. Just follow the signs."

"Thanks," Alex and London say at the same time and take off to change so they can join the other teens in the pool.

"TiTi Né! Uncle James!" Maya and Aaliyah yell as they enter the same doors my kids just walked through. They give us a quick hug before heading off again.

So, this TiTi Né thing is a thing? Cool.

"James, I think Allen is inside preparing the meat," Nelle says.

I totally picked up on that code language: go inside and leave us girls alone. Yup, I like her.

"Cool. I'll go check him out." James gives me a kiss and heads inside.

"Drink?" Nelle says.

"Absolutely."

As she fixes the drinks, Nelle has a way of having a conversation without having one. "I know things have been tense between you and Derrick, but I think it's because you guys are so much alike."

Are we, though? How could she think that we

are so much alike? We weren't even raised in the same state, let alone in the same house or even by the same mother.

"Either way," Nelle continues. "Today is about fun and chill and there's plenty of space for y'all not to be in each other's space." As she winks, she gives what should be a comforting smile.

Is there, though? Enough space?

"So, tell me all about Atlanta! Nelle continues as if she didn't just drop a bomb on me and there's no mess to clean up from the emotional explosion. I play along because she said there's enough space, so I should have nothing to worry about. "I've been trying to get Allen to move there for years! I'm hoping that when AJ goes to college, I can finally convince Allen to move. So, how's the traffic?" she asks, halting the internal argument that I am having with myself.

Nelle continues as if she didn't just drop a bomb on me and there's no mess to clean up from the emotional explosion. I play along because she said there's enough space so I should have nothing to worry about.

"Girl, the traffic is horrible! There are so many cars and people all the time. And everyone drives so fast."

The conversation between Nelle and I continues like this for a while. It feels good to be relaxed and just have girl talk. I guess this is the benefit to having a sister-in-law.

The kids are off having fun in the pool. The guys are cooking, and I am enjoying the drinks and conversation.

A simple family dinner with enough space.

"Meat's off the grill. Everyone come eat!" Allen announces from the doorway "Kids, everything is set up for y'all downstairs in the basement. Adults, this way," he says as he ushers us through a large doorway.

"Hey, sis," Allen says and hugs me as I approach.

"Hey, Allen." I say as I walk through the door, looking around cautiously.

I see James already fixing me a plate. I smile at the way he takes care of me.

And then I spot him, Derrick. My whole attitude changes. I can feel my smile turn into a smirk and I subconsciously fold my arms.

There's enough room. I keep repeating to myself in my head. There's enough room. There's enough room.

That's what Nelle said but this room is feeling mighty small right now.

"Hey, Renee," Derrick says with a semi-genuine tone.

"Hey, Derrick," I reply back, trying to hide the

angst in my voice.

"Babe, I started making your plate," James says, rescuing me from this awkward interaction.

"Allen, I'm so glad you burnt a few hot dogs. That's my favorite way to eat them," I comment as I squeeze ketchup and relish in just the right proportions over my nicely burnt hot dog.

"Yeah, James made sure that I got a few nice and crispy for you," Allen replies. "He does a great job of looking out for you."

"That he does," I reply and wink at James. Always my protector.

With our plates fixed and drinks in hand, we head toward the dinner table for what smells like an amazing meal.

As we enjoy our food, music plays in the background and all you can hear in the room is people smacking on their barbecue. Allen outdid himself with this! I am sure that James' help consisted of him talking sports and drinking beers with the guys.

I hold up my rib bone, "Allen, you did a good job, this rib is so darn good."

Nelle, Allen and I start to laugh hysterically remembering James' iconic moment in the restaurant.

Derrick looks around, confused by the sudden outcry of laughter.

Through tears and laughter, Allen explains the scene from the other day.

Derrick's look changes from confusion to a combination of something that I can't quite put my finger on. Is it frustration? Is it exclusion? Is it sadness? Is it anger?

Derrick eventually shrugs his shoulders and says, "I guess you had to be there."

Through tearful giggles, Nelle adds, "Yeah, bro. It was a classic moment."

We continue eating, drinking, talking and laughing. The atmosphere is light and friendly. Surprisingly.

"Renee, James, do you guys know how to play spades?" Allen asks as Nelle and I clear the table.

"Do we? Are you serious? Of course, we know how to play spades. Just name the rules," James replies rather confidently.

"Big joker, little joker, Ace of Spades," Allen declares as he intensely shuffles the cards.

Spades is a long-standing tradition of sorts at most Southern barbecues. When the drinks flow and music plays, a spades game must eventually commence.

Just as the cards are pulled out, and Allen and Nelle take a seat at the table, James announces, "I think I am going to sit out this hand."

What the hell did my husband just say? I sit

back trying to make sure that I heard him correctly.

James continues, "Derrick will you partner with Renee?" My husband's face is stone serious, as if he thinks I don't know what he is attempting to do.

"Well…" Derrick begins, obviously hesitant.

"Have a seat, Derrick. It doesn't matter who your partner is; my wife and I are going to whoop your butts anyways," Allen assertively announces, cutting Derrick off mid-sentence.

"Sit on down, Derrick, and let's show these fools what we got," I say, trying to sound equally confident. Internally, I am freaking out. I am convinced that James and Allen set this up. Probably while they were cooking the food.

So much for being patient.

Spades has a way of bringing people together through trash talking and fun competition. We've played several rounds of cards. At first, things were awkward between Derrick and me, but we slowly started to ease into a good routine and we're actually having fun. We're not best friends by any means but we're trash talking Allen and Nelle while winning more than losing.

James checks on the kids, who are having a ball downstairs. He delivers a "status report" on the children's activities to ease our nerves. The girls are doing Tik Tok challenges and Alex and AJ are playing the latest Madden game. "Overall, everyone is having a great time," James states and takes a sip of his drink.

We continue to play Spades. I play the last card of the hand.

"Renee, you cut my King," Derrick states rather harshly, a stark contrast to his attitude a few minutes ago.

Okay, Derrick played a King that could have won the hand, but I had no choice but to play an Ace which is higher than his. That shouldn't matter though, because we're partners.

"Yeah, I didn't have a choice. Sorry but we set them so it's all good."

For my non-spades players, each team of two guesses how many cards they can win over everyone else. Being "set" means the other team didn't win as many cards as they guessed they would. So, we won. But that doesn't matter to grumpy over here.

"Of course, it's all good," Derrick hisses, each word dripping with angry venom. "Because Goody Two Shoes Renee said so, I guess."

"Whoa, not that serious. It was a play. We're winning. Calm down," I reply trying to ignore the "goody two shoe" remark and be the bigger person. I'm not sure who Derrick is used to talking to, but he is not about to talk crazy to me.

James has moved a little closer to the table but is still sipping his drink and observing.

Derrick obviously hasn't picked up on my attempt to calm the situation. He continues down his path of self-destruction. "You know, you think you can waltz in here, pay the dinner bill, give your fake Boston smile and everyone is supposed to just accept what you're saying, huh?"

"Hold up, Bro. It's just a game," Allen interjects, trying to calm things down at the table.

"I'm not talking about no damn game. I'm talking about how this chick thinks she's better than all of us." Derrick stands up, slamming his chair into the cabinet behind him as he continues, "No one cares about your perfect family. No one cares that you laugh like Virginia. No one cares that you had the perfect childhood."

"Hold up, Derrick," James begins to interject as he has strategically moved right behind me, letting me know that he has my back one hundred percent.

I cut him off to respond to this fool's accusations. "I got this, James. Hold the fuck up, Derrick! I'm not sure who you thought I was, but your last statement shows that you don't know a damn thing about me! Perfect childhood? That's just laughable." My words are covered with disdain, hate and disgust. I continue, "How about instead of spending all of your time drinking you learn who the hell I am. My husband and I work really hard for the things we have. So, if we want to splurge and pay for a few dinners, we will. And I don't laugh like Virginia, I laugh like Renee."

I stand, looking around to grab whatever the hell I brought into this house: my phone, keys and anything else. I give James the look that lets him know it is time to go before I really tell Derrick about himself.

I barely hear Allen and Nelle in the background trying to calm everyone down, but the damage has been done. Allen has moved in front of Derrick, hopefully to talk some sense into him.

James yells for the kids to grab their stuff because we're leaving.

I'm glad he was able to appropriately read my body language because I am holding my tongue, fearing what may come out at any moment.

"Oh yeah," I turn for one last statement, "your coat is on fire. Who wears a damn down jacket in the middle of the summer? Get your shit together."

Just then the room fills with down feathers from Derrick's puffy jacket. In his haste to "tell me about myself" he stood a little too close to one of Nelle's candles that was on the cabinet behind him. And now, his down feathers are flying everywhere.

Serves his ass right!

Derrick snatches his jacket off, hitting it repeatedly attempting to put out the small flames. With each hit to save his jacket, more feathers come flying until he is surrounded in a cloud of feathers.

The kids come upstairs, confused by the sudden call to leave and the feathers flying everywhere.

"But dad, we were making another video," London protests.

"And I was finally beating AJ in Madden," Alex adds in.

"Alex and London," I say through clenched teeth "say goodbye and get in the car."

Both children take note of the tense environment and oblige. We say goodnight over our shoulders as we head out the door and to the car. James opens my car door to let me in; ensuring no more damage is done.

There wasn't enough room.

We head to the hotel and no one speaks the entire drive.

When we arrive, before James can shut off the car, I place my hand on his, "I need to go for a drive, clear my mind."

He nods, kisses me on my forehead and exits the car with our kids. He sends the kids into the hotel without him and walks over to the driver side window as I buckle in and adjust the mirrors.

James places his hands on the window's ledge "Drive Safe," he says leaning in to kiss my forehead.

"I will. Promise," I reply.

***

CHAPTER 11

Thank God for silence. Just me, the open road and my thoughts. I thought I was doing the right thing by coming to Memphis. But at this moment, I think the past is dragging me down.

I need to process all that happened tonight. The yelling, the name calling, and the accusations being thrown around like a football on a Sunday afternoon. I don't know where it all went wrong, and honestly, I don't care. I'm just glad to be here and not there.

I laugh like Virginia. Perfect childhood.

That dude is living in an alternate reality.

Ugh! I can't believe I let myself lose control like that. I wouldn't be surprised if Dr. C is disappointed in me when I get back and tell her how my effort at "bridging the gap" went.

I can see the serious look on her face as she tries to delve deeper into understanding the situation. "Okay, but did you hear him out? How do you think you could have listened to his side of the story before leaving?" I can hear Dr. C asking me about the experience. Being sure not to ask me a *yes* or *no* question to keep the conversation flowing. Dr. C wouldn't scold me, even though I may deserve it a little bit. Should I have heard him out? Hell no!

I'd had enough of Derrick and his condescending ass.

The dark highway wraps up my anger in a nice little bow and the darkness surrounds me, providing a blanket of comfort.

Derrick has no idea the hell I went through as a child raising an alcoholic parent. How dare he judge James and me for working to provide a different life for our children?

He has no idea of the baggage that I carried with me everywhere for so long. The baggage was enough to fit into one of those big purses most women down south carry. I carried this baggage until last year, when I started working towards healing.

That pompous bastard doesn't have to worry

about ever being in my presence again. My family and I will spend our last few days enjoying what Memphis has to offer without him and his wrong-as-hell accusations.

I turn the radio up, zone out and drive a bit farther. I need to make a quick stop at Chick-Fil-A for apology shakes before heading back to the hotel. There's nothing like saying "I'm sorry I went off on Virginia's douchebag son and had to leave so abruptly." than with Chick-fil-A milkshakes.

I knew the house wasn't big enough.

***

"Hey, Sis," I hear as I pick up the phone.

"What's up, Allen?" I say, obviously annoyed. Allen's the one who keeps surprising me with Derrick's presence, so he's partly to blame for last night.

"I want to apologize for last night. Can you meet me for lunch? Just you and I—no one else."

Hesitantly, and for reasons I don't understand, I reply "sure," with a slight eye roll that he can't see. While gathering my purse and keys, I tell my family that I am headed to meet him.

James and the kids are going to lunch in the hotel. Alex and London have already started talking in their fake English accents. James laughs at the kids and kisses me on the forehead.

"I'll be back soon. I don't plan on this being a long conversation, so I should be in and out," I tell James as I try to delay the uncomfortable situation that waits in the future.

"Take your time. London has some shopping she wants to do, and I am sure Alex will find some sneakers to add to his ridiculous collection. Have an open mind, Renee," James tells me as he closes the car door.

"I'm trying, James," I reply and drive off.

I really am — trying. Driving to God-knows-where to have lunch with Allen and *talk.*

"Magic Wings and Things," I read the sign outside of the building for the address Allen gave me. I'm hoping the food will be worth the drive. Everything else is yet to be seen.

"Did we have to come all this way for lunch?" I ask Allen as I get out of the car.

"Hey, Sis. I wanted you to see some of the different neighborhoods. This is 'Whitehaven,'" Allen replies as he attempts to hug me. We're definitely back to the awkward hug stage again.

"What's so special about Whitehaven?"

"Whitehaven is where black people flocked to back in the day. It's now filled with middle-class working families who take a lot of pride in protecting our history. Let's go inside and get some food."

Lemon Pepper wings and something called "Philly fries" adorn my plate as we find a quiet booth in the corner.

"We finally finished picking up all of the feathers," Allen says, attempting to make light of the obviously explosive ending to yesterday's event. "Renee, let me start off by saying I'm sorry for inviting Derrick to dinner the first night and not telling you."

"The first night?" I say with my head cocked to the side, lip curled on one end, eyes big and concerning.

"Let me finish. I had good intentions. I know you two struggle and I thought it would be easier if it was in a public place versus privately."

"Yeah, because privately worked so well yesterday," I reply, snarky as hell.

"You two are so much alike; that's why you're always going at each other."

"First of all, you and Nelle need to stop with that. Second of all, no, we're not. Derrick has no idea what my childhood was like. He's made a bunch of assumptions and miscategorized my family and me. We're not perfect, nor do we think we are. But we love each other and our kids and work hard not to recreate the past."

"You may be right, Renee, but you both have

assumptions about each other."

I look at him, perplexed. *What assumptions have I made about Derrick? None, that's what.* "Allen, y'all were living the best life in Alabama with your grandparents. I was in Boston fending for myself."

"Renee, we didn't stay in Alabama with Grandma and Grandpa. And what do you mean 'fending for yourself?'"

Why must he ask questions that I really don't want to answer? It's only going to make this lunch that much more uncomfortable.

We both eat in silence as we work to understand the realness of the situation that was just revealed.

So, they didn't grow up in Alabama? And he clearly doesn't know about Virginia's drinking? This is too much.

"Let's go for a walk," Allen says as we throw our trash away.

***

CHAPTER 12

We sit in a park surrounded by some of the largest and most gorgeous trees I have ever seen. I close my eyes, allow the sun to warm my face and attempt to appreciate this quiet moment with nature.

"Did you know that I came to Boston before? I was going to move there after eighth grade." Allen breaks the silence.

"Really?"

"Yeah. When our grandparents realized Momma left Derrick and me alone, of course they moved us in with them. Months later, Momma had come down for my eighth-grade graduation. You hadn't been born yet. I don't even think she knew she was pregnant. Anyhow, she came down for my graduation and was so proud to tell Grandma and Grandpa that she had found a good man and was making a good life for herself in Boston. Grandpa, Grandma and Momma had a huge argument. I was eavesdropping from the hallway so I couldn't hear everything, but it was something about her always jumping from man to man and leaving her kids."

Isn't that ironic? I think to myself.

"She left the next day and told Derrick and me that we were welcomed if we wanted to come to Boston. A few months later, I convinced Grandma and Grandpa that I wanted to move to Boston to be with Momma, so I did.

"I remember that your dad was cool. He used to smoke cigars in the backyard, and we would just talk. By the time I got there, Momma realized she was pregnant with you. Boston was cool but it didn't feel right. The buses. The noise. The concrete everywhere; it was so different from Alabama. I spent a month or so there before I begged her to send me back. I didn't have to beg hard."

By the look in Allen's eyes, it's as if he is remembering how the 14-year-old felt when he returned back to Alabama without his mother.

"When I got back," Allen continues, " Derrick was so angry with me. He thought I was abandoning him like Momma had abandoned us both. But he didn't stay mad too long. Especially when Grandma and Grandpa moved us to Memphis with Auntie Donna."

"I vaguely remember her from the funeral," I say. "I didn't even know Virginia had a sister or that you guys lived with her!"

"Auntie Donna was younger than Momma and still living at home. I remember she used to sleep in late and go out partying all night. Grandpa and Auntie Donna would argue constantly. Auntie Donna thought she was being punished for Momma's wrongdoings and often said that Grandma and Grandpa loved Momma more.

"Eventually, the arguments became more than anyone wanted to deal with anymore. One argument got really bad, and Auntie Donna left Grandma and Grandpa's house and headed to live in Memphis.

"Auntie Donna became yet another person who left Derrick and me behind. When she left, Derrick began to act out. Grandma and Grandpa were getting old and raising two teenage boys, one who was angrier than a crying baby waiting for their bottle to warm. It was not what my grandparents had planned for their retirement. So, off to Memphis Derrick and I went.

"Auntie Donna is the coolest. She really looked

out for Derrick and me. Auntie Donna never made us feel unwanted or unloved. In fact, she did everything she could to make sure we were taken care of and she made sure our education came first. During the week, Auntie Donna worked a regular nine to five at a small, local packaging company. She checked our homework at night and always had a hot meal on the stove for us. But the weekends were a completely different version of Auntie Donna."

"How so?" I ask, leaning forward on the edge of the park bench.

"She loved to entertain and party. That didn't change just because Derrick and I moved in. Almost every weekend, the basement was jumping at Auntie's house. Of course, Derrick and I were restricted to our bedroom upstairs, so we didn't join in on the adult fun. But we definitely enjoyed listening to the music.

"Derrick and I cracked up laughing when everyone joined together in a drunken chorus to sing the signature line from Frankie Beverly and Maze's *Before I Let Go.* Allen chuckles at what are clearly good memories.

"After high school, I went to the University of Memphis. I wanted to play basketball and eventually go into the NBA, but my knees had other ideas for me. I majored in Political Science and focused my attention on Law School. During my junior year, I did a year of 'studying abroad' at Howard. That's where I met Nelle, and the rest is history."

"What about Derrick?" I interject. "What was happening with him during this time?"

"Derrick graduated from high school two years before me, moved out and started working. College life wasn't really for him. He found a good job at General Electric and lived life the best way he knew how. If you ask me, he never really got over Momma leaving."

Silence falls between Allen and me. The breeze gently blows carrying sounds of children playing in the far-off distance. The leaves on the trees move with the breeze creating a medley of peace and tranquility. The complete opposite of my internal feelings after learning so much about Allen's upbringing.

After a while, he continues, "Derrick doesn't hate you Renee. He's just trying to find a reason for Momma leaving us. Her leaving for a few days wasn't anything new to us; she would leave for a few days here or there. But she always returned. My grandparents said that she left when she met my dad, but when she returned that time she was pregnant with me.

"When momma got pregnant with me, she

realized it was time for her to find a place of her own. When we moved out of Grandma and Grandpa's house into our own place, it wasn't big and fancy, but it was ours and things were good for Derrick, Momma and me. Until they weren't.

"When she left the last time, it was different. Even her return was different; this time, she didn't come back to Grandma and Grandpa's to get us. It felt like she came back to tell us she was moving on.

"As the older brother, the responsibility always falls on Derrick to take care of me. Then I turned around and left him, too.

"But you came back," I remind him.

"Yeah, but *she* never did. She chose you and the life she was living in Boston."

Wow. That's deep. "I'm sorry that she walked out on you guys," I tell Allen. "Maybe it was for the better. At least you had biological relatives in your life who were able to take care of you both. I had an Easy Bake oven and a generous neighbor."

"What happened up there? What did you mean when you said you had to fend for yourself?" Allen asks, his eyes searching for understanding while hiding beneath pain.

"How much time do you have?" I say back and give an uneasy chuckle. "Seriously, Virginia tried to raise me, but she had a true addiction. She was an alcoholic and I wasn't old enough to help her overcome it. When my father left, I had to fend for myself until I was rescued."

"Renee, may I ask you a question?"

"*Now*, you want to ask for permission?" I say sarcastically.

"I noticed that you call Momma 'Virginia.' Why?"

"Maybe because she walked out on me too. Not physically but definitely mentally."

Allen nods accepting the realness of my words.

We both sit in silence and the sun contains to radiate on my face showering me in natural vitamin C.

"I wish I would have been there for you, Renee. I wish you didn't have to fend for yourself," Allen says quietly. "I wish she hadn't left you and that we had a chance to build a relationship from the beginning."

"Let's start now. Let's continue to bridge the gap and allow our kids to know each other." I say throwing in Dr. C's favorite phrase for my healing journey.

"I think that's a great idea; Alex and AJ get along so well. And Nelle pays so much attention to London's projects," Allen adds, leaning his head against mine. "It would be nice if we could *all* bridge the gap, Renee."

I roll my eyes as I catch the emphasis on the word "all." I know what he means and I'm not feeling it. "After last night, which I apologize for—I shouldn't have lost my temper like that—but I think it's safe to say that Derrick and I will never get to where you and I are."

"I think you guys just need to hear each other out."

"You mean over the alcohol, cold, defensive body language and smart-ass comments?" I respond back with a snotty attitude that would rival any teenage girl.

Allen gives me a look that clearly reads "enough."

"Maybe y'all could go for appetizers or something. I know a full meal is a stretch," Allen replies attempting to extend an olive branch.

"Maybe," I say, but I'm not even convinced by my statement.

Allen and I sit enjoying the scene around us as the sun begins to journey past the highest point in the sky signaling the change to later afternoon. We've been here much longer than either of us expected.

"Should we head back to the car?" Allen asks breaking my thoughts.

"Yeah, I should get back to James and the kids. We have dinner plans tonight."

As we walk back to the car and head to the restaurant where I left my rental, there is a heaviness between us. A sadness of sorts. Unresolved feelings of abandonment that have resurfaced.

"I love you, little sister, and I am so glad that you came to Memphis so I could meet my brother-in-law, niece and nephew."

"I love you, too, Allen. AJ is such a special kid and Nelle is a bundle of joy, who hugs a little too tightly but she's still cool."

"Yeah, that's kind of her thing. Keeping everyone close to her."

Allen laughs and before we part ways, we hug. As I head back toward the hotel, the awkwardness between Allen and me is gone and I feel exposed. I feel vulnerable and weak from the rehashing of memories from which I was working so hard to heal. It's clear to me now that we both have healing work to do.

***

CHAPTER 13

"I was 16 when she left. Did you know that?" Derrick says as he takes a sip of his drink.

Allen set up a lunch for Derrick and me to talk. I arrived early and requested the knives to be removed from the table. Don't judge me. I know Allen said Derrick doesn't hate me but just in case.

"No, I didn't know that until my conversation with Allen," I reply, trying not to sound angry, annoyed or sarcastic.

"I tried to keep the house going. Made sure Allen went to school. Picked up odd jobs. Cooked whatever food was left in the pantry and fridge. But the food ran out and I had to go to my grandparents for help. I hated asking them. I should have been able to provide for him until she came back. She always came back, eventually."

"You were waiting for her?"

"Yeah! She had disappeared before but never for long. I never knew where she went, and I was a child, so I didn't question her actions. But this time was different; I had no idea she was off building her *dream life* in Boston."

I chuckle at the word "dream." If only he knew how much of a nightmare it was. "Sorry." I say and shrug my shoulders.

"I lost track of how long she had been gone before she returned. We had finally gotten into a routine with Grandma and Grandpa. One day, we come in from school and she was at the house, sitting on the couch with a big smile on her face and arms open for a hug. Allen was so happy to see her, the happiest I saw him in a long time. Virginia spent the whole night bragging about her fancy Boston life and her new man. She didn't even bother to ask if I was okay. She sat there and pretended like everything was okay, sashaying into town and talking about how amazing Boston was. Our grandparents weren't happy about her being there. I could tell. I felt the same way, I couldn't stand to even look at her. When Grandma and Grandpa eventually told us to get ready for bed, the look on Allen's face went from absolute glee to fear.

"He was so scared that he would go to bed and she wouldn't be there when he woke up. She must have noticed something was wrong because that's when she had the nerve to offer us a trip to Boston." Hunched over his drink, in a soft melancholic tone, Derrick continues, "Allen took her up on the offer and he left me, too."

"That was the first time I got in trouble for drinking. Grandpa was so mad when his beers went missing. But what was he going to do besides yell? I was bigger than him, faster than him and obviously younger than him. He finally realized that I wasn't a little boy anymore. I can admit that I started to 'smell myself' as Grandma would say. Looking back now, I can honestly say that I caused a little more trouble than Grandpa and Grandma deserved. I can see why they shipped us off to Auntie Donna's when Allen came back." Derrick speaks his final words with a hint of sadness.

In this moment, I can feel his pain. His hurt. His feeling of abandonment. What he went through had to be a heavy burden for a 16-year-old to carry. So much hurt and pain that the grown man sitting with me is still carrying it.

We sit in silence for a while before Derrick speaks again. "Auntie Donna wasn't expecting us to show up at her house. She was younger than

Virginia and still enjoying life. Because I was older, she told me she wasn't going to be the 'strict' aunt. I didn't need her to be strict or cool. I didn't need anything. I moved out as soon as I graduated from high school. I got a good job at General Electric to pay the bills, married Robin and I was going to live the life Virginia never gave me. Well, obviously things didn't work out with Robin. She got fed up with my occasional run-ins with the law. I got tired of her accusing me of having a drinking problem. Our relationship didn't work but we made two beautiful little girls, so I guess something good came out of it."

We both call her "Virginia." Interesting.

There's a sense of happiness in his voice as he talks about Maya and Aaliyah. I think I even see a slight smile. His love for his daughters is clear. But then his mood changes. The smile disappears and a hardness takes over his face. "I like to have a few drinks but I'm not a drunk. I go to work every day and I provide for my girls." He says defensively.

"Virginia was an alcoholic," I tell Derrick, "and I believe you are a functioning alcoholic."

Derrick stares at me, confused but appearing to want to hear more before he jumps down my throat.

So I carefully continue, "I don't know why, but I think Virginia used alcohol to mask her pain and

I think you may be doing the same thing."

"I don't have no damn pain! The woman left. So what?" His words are wrapped in anger and pain. He sits at the table with squared shoulders and a deep intensity in his eyes.

"*So what?* We both call the woman who gave us life by her first name; dude, you and I both have pain."

There's a long silence again. Derrick continues to stare into the empty glass in front of him as if he's looking for an answer. We both nibble on the appetizers, thinking about all that was just shared.

"I don't hate you Renee," Derrick says, breaking the silence. "I just hate that you had her and we didn't."

"You and Allen both think that I had Virginia," I lean back in my seat, head tilted to the side, trying to contain myself before I continue. "You are correct, she was physically in Boston. In the same state as me. But I didn't really *have* her.

"Derrick, she may have physically been there, but most of the time she wasn't there because of the alcohol. It was actually quite lonely and all I could think about when I found out that I had two older brothers and grandparents was 'Why don't they save me from this woman?' But now I realize, you can't save someone you don't know needs saving."

Silence settles again and I'm sure Derrick is processing just like I am.

"Virginia did a great job of selling you, Allen and your grandparents on a story that wasn't true," I tell Derrick matter-of-factly. "Her life in Boston wasn't a dream and it definitely wasn't perfect. But I am sure that was obvious when you came up for the funeral."

Derrick grunts in agreement and shrugs his shoulders. "The funeral? Yeah. The funeral."

"What does that mean?" I ask, sensing Derrick's sarcasm or disbelief. I can't tell which one.

"It was like we were spectators instead of her sons. I felt like the whole thing was planned and no one asked Allen or me what we wanted. You all just buried Virginia in that unmarked grave like she didn't matter. And after we left the cemetery, you just disappeared."

I think back to that day, a day I don't like to think about or remember. A day I try to bury deep inside and hide away.

Derrick's right. I couldn't handle all of the newfound family members, burying the person who gave me life and thinking I failed her and her sobriety. I left the cemetery and took off. I sent text messages to those who mattered, letting them know that I needed some space and wanted to clear my head. Allen, Derrick and Donna were not among that group. I didn't know them; I didn't owe them an explanation as to why I wouldn't be around for the "repass" surrounded by strangers.

"Renee?"

"Sorry," I say as I let the memories fade away. "I knew of you and Allen, but I didn't *know* you guys. I was young and writing the obituary of a woman I barely knew. I was also a college student, so an unmarked grave was my only option."

And I didn't see you or Allen opening your wallets during the service, I think to myself. *I'm not sure if I want to even open this can or worms, but here goes nothing.*

"May I ask you a question?" I cautiously ask.

"Sure," Derrick answers hesitantly.

"At the funeral, I remember you staring at me. Almost like you were ready to rip my head off." Goosebumps run down my arms as I remember that moment.

"Sorry, I wasn't intentionally meaning to stare at you. I just remember sitting there and being confused and angry. I didn't understand how we ended up there. I hadn't spoken to Virginia in months. But she seemed happy, and she always said that everything was okay." Derrick looks into his glass as he says these words; seemingly still trying to come to terms.

"Well, I was right here, and I was surprised, too. I thought she was sober, but she wasn't. I found bottles hidden in the craziest spots when I cleaned up her apartment. She had been hiding her drinking and I had no idea. I failed to keep her sober."

Derrick leans back, tilts his head to the side and asks, "You cleaned up her apartment?"

"Yeah," *Someone had to.* "Shortly after the funeral," I reply.

"I imagine you had to do a lot of stuff that adults should have taken care of for you." Derrick says with a hint of pity.

"I guess, but I just did what I needed to do."

Heavy silence. Feelings of unnecessary guilt and lots of confusion are floating in the air making the room uncomfortable.

"I'm sorry, Renee."

"Yeah, me too, Derrick."

More silence. The air in the room still uncomfortable but more filled with sadness than anger or guilt.

"Derrick. Please don't take offense to what I am about to suggest."

He grunts, "Okay."

"I think you need to see a counselor. I started last year after my trip to Boston. It has helped me to dissect all the feelings that I had once we returned home from our trip."

Derrick doesn't immediately respond. "A counselor? Like lying on a couch and telling someone all of my problems?"

I chuckle. "Nah, I sit in a chair, we eat bon bons and talk about the latest episode of *Real Housewives*."

We both laugh at the thought.

"Seriously, I found an incredibly kind and attentive therapist who tells me like it is. It's really helped." *This conversation is proof that therapy has worked.*

"I'll think about it," he replies to my surprise.

We finish the appetizers and drinks in silence.

"Thank you for meeting me. I know I've been an ass."

"Yeah, you have," I say and chuckle. "I think we were both being an ass at some point or another."

"Truce?" Derrick asks with a hint of a smile and hopefulness in his eyes.

"Truce." I nod in agreement.

As we get up to leave, there's an awkward moment between us. *Do we hug or no?*

"Maybe a pound," Derrick says, reading my mind.

"Yeah, let's pound it out," I say with a slight smile.

Derrick and I get into our cars and head to our

respective destinations. Maybe, just maybe I can bridge this gap between us. When I first arrived at the restaurant, I didn't think I would walk away from having appetizers and drinks with Virginia's son with a renewed feeling of hope. But I am.

Dr. C would definitely be proud of me.

***

I return to the hotel feeling a little lighter than before I left.

I've spent the last twenty minutes or so snuggled with James, detailing my interesting afternoon lunch. He's been pretty quiet and listening attentively.

"Renee, I am very proud of you. Sounds like you had a breakthrough," James finally says.

"Yeah, it was a decent way to end the trip." I snuggle up closer to my hubby.

"I'm glad," James says as he kisses my forehead.

I am so blessed that I found James. This man is always my protector, being there to make sure I am safe, mentally and physically, through all of life's challenges. James does an amazing job providing for our family, so my security is never in question. Hmph.

Before this weekend, I would have said that

James is the complete opposite of both Allen and Derrick. But after spending some time with them, I know that they love their families and want the best for the people in their lives. I guess my brothers aren't much different from my husband after all.

Interesting.

***

CHAPTER 14

"TiTi Né! Uncle James! Over here," Maya and Aaliyah yell in unison.

James, the kids and I decided to spend our last night in Memphis doing dinner at the Brazilian restaurant again.

As we join my brothers and their families at the table, we exchange kisses on cheeks, hugs, pounds and secret handshakes. This dinner feels more comfortable. The atmosphere is more relaxed, no tension in the room. The smiles are real. The conversations are genuine. And there are less drinks flowing tonight.

Maybe Derrick did listen to me earlier.

Once again, AJ and Alex have successfully

attempted to eat all of the meat in the entire restaurant, and at the end of our meal, our server bids us a farewell and thanks us for joining them tonight.

The adults at the table have fallen eerily quiet in comparison to a few moments ago. We look around at each other, confused; the server never brought our bill.

Just as James raises his hand, Derrick smiles and says, "I got it tonight brother-in-law. My treat."

"Well, damn," Allen says. "I wish I would have known you were paying; I would have added the lobster."

We all laugh, including Derrick.

After exiting the restaurant and heading for our cars, the kids are huddled over to the side, obviously plotting; I'm sure we'll figure out what *that* is about later. As my family exchanges their goodbyes, I can't believe—and I'm scared to comment aloud—but my brothers and I may have actually succeeded in beginning to bridge our deep-rooted and long-avoided gap.

There is still work to be done both individually and as siblings, but as I watch my brothers interact with my husband and kids, I feel like I can actually see and feel the foundation we're laying. If Dr. C were here watching us, I'm sure she'd make a comment about the we've made progress. I am confident that we will continue to do the work to understand the past and shape the future of our relationship.

***

EPILOGUE

It's a cool, September afternoon. The leaves on the trees are starting to change to beautiful reds, oranges and yellows.

My family and I—my brothers and their families included—decided Labor Day weekend was a good time to come up to Boston. Before the temperature dropped too drastically.

As my brothers, sister-in-law, and I gather closely together, there aren't many words being shared. We stand silently gazing at the large stone monument that stands before us.

Virginia Watson Lee
January 10, 1944 – October 20, 2000
Mother, Magician, Traveler

Last year, my brothers and I video-called the cemetery and chose a stone that we felt like matched the different personas of who Virginia was to us. We decided these three words described her very well. She was our mother, she was great at disappearing, and she loved to travel and meet new people.

As I stand with my brothers next to me and take in this moment, I smile slightly and a tear trickles down my cheek. I never imagined this scenario happening. But it has. My brothers, no longer Virginia's kids, and I are together in Boston. We've come together to heal old wounds. To put the past behind us and no longer carry the baggage that resulted from truths hurt feelings, abandonment and assumptions. We've respectfully spoken our truths and we are bridging the gap to make new memories. Together.

Today, we stand and admire our mother's final resting place. We have all been in town for the last few days, sightseeing and preparing for this moment. The kids, Alex, London, Maya and Aaliyah, join us after a few moments, each holding a bouquet of peace lilies for their grandmother's new gravestone. Alex is holding an extra bouquet for AJ who couldn't miss classes at the University of Memphis to be here.

"TiTi Né, Alex said the lobsters will have eyes,"

Maya says, her tone and facial expressions showing she is clearly disgusted. We're headed to dinner after we leave here; I guess the kids have been discussing it while they waited in the car.

"We can have them take the heads off before they bring them to the table," I reply, rolling my eyes at Alex.

"Uncle Allen and Uncle Derrick, did you know that Ms. Virginia used to roll her hair with brown paper bags?" London shares.

"Why'd she do that?" asks Maya, with her face scrunched up, looking confused.

"That's so weird," Aaliyah replies.

"Yeah, she used to do that when I was little, too. I forgot all about that," Derrick says with a grin on his face.

"Me, too." Allen nods in agreement.

"On that note," I say, interrupting all of our reminiscing, "let's head back to our cars and go have some dinner. Who's in the mood for lobster eyeballs?"

***

Kim, my father's wife, and I have been talking a lot lately. The phone rings and wakes me up from a light sleep. I've been anticipating this call for a while.

"Renee, it's time," Kim says on the other end of the phone.

"Okay, I'm on my way," I say groggily.

***

ACKNOWLEDGEMENTS

I want to give the most high praise to my Lord and Savior Jesus Christ for the visions and gifts that you have blessed me with for the purpose of spreading love.

I want to thank my husband who is the yin to my yang. Thank you for supporting me and allowing me to chase my dreams.

To my loudest cheerleader, Jaden Carter, thank you! Y'all, this boy will tell everyone and their momma about my book. He's like my mini publicist whom I pay in the form of food. Mommy loves you, J. Carter!

To my Mommy, Kletus, Mom Carole, Coby/Earl/Brea family, and all of my family —

thank you for continuing to encourage me to be extraordinary.

My Beta readers, Courtney, Trafonda, and Amanda, y'all are the real rock stars! Y'all really helped me to shape this book. Thank you for taking the time to help me create a better product.

Mandy, we did it again! I still can't explain how much you mean to me as an author, friend, and sister. You push me and make me better. Your willingness to teach me along the way is appreciated more than I can say!

I would be remiss not to shout out my cousin Marc for all things Memphis. Thank you for sharing your beautiful city with me to create the perfect backdrop for this book.

There are so many people who have encouraged and supported me along the way. I am so grateful to all of them. My sisters, brother, sistercousins, brothercousins, nieces, nephews, aunties, uncles, and everyone else — y'all are the reason I keep going.

And finally, the reader, I wouldn't be here without you. Renee is a complicated character and I hope that you enjoy her journey as she bridges the gap.

ABOUT THE AUTHOR

Maria Anderson was born and raised in Boston, Massachusetts. Her faith is her foundation and her family is her motivation. She is a foodie who loves trying new restaurants, food trucks or anywhere with a good taco! Maria loves to travel, especially to warmer climates that have drinks with umbrellas, and she loves spending time with friends and family making memories and living life to the fullest. Maria also owns an event planning business, Center of Attention, where she celebrates life's most precious moments and makes her clients the center of attention on their special day.

Maria currently lives in Florida with her husband and son. *The Other Side of Fear Trilogy* is available on Amazon.